FACT: You won't want to miss a single one!!!

#1 LOUISE TRAPEZE IS TOTALLY 100% FEARLESS

COMING SOON:

**#2 LOUISE TRAPEZE DID NOT LOSE
THE JUGGLING CHICKENS**

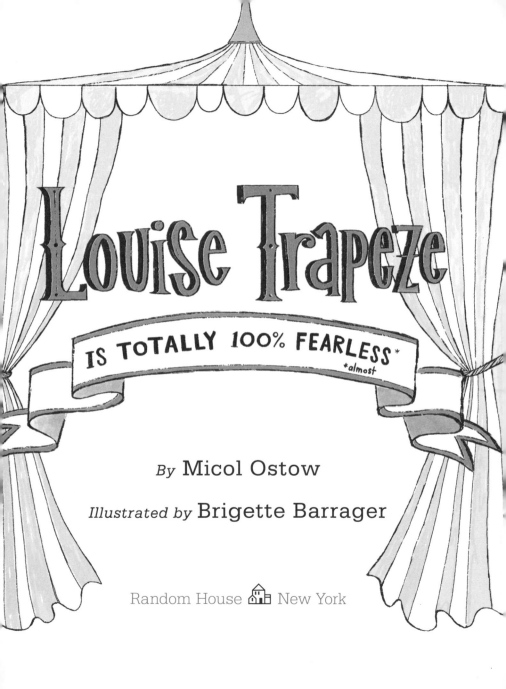

Louise Trapeze

IS TOTALLY 100% FEARLESS *
almost

By Micol Ostow

Illustrated by Brigette Barrager

Random House 🏠 New York

FOR MAZZY, MY EXTRA-FEARLESS SHINING STAR

Text copyright © 2015 by Micol Ostow
Jacket art and interior illustrations copyright © 2015 by Brigette Barrager

Visit us on the Web! randomhousekids.com

Educators and librarians, for a variety of teaching tools,
visit us at RHTeachersLibrarians.com

Library of Congress Cataloging-in-Publication Data
Ostow, Micol.
Louise Trapeze is totally 100% fearless / Micol Ostow ;
illustrated by Brigette Barrager. — First edition.
pages cm.
ISBN 978-0-553-49739-7 (trade) — ISBN 978-0-553-49740-3 (lib. bdg.) —
ISBN 978-0-553-49741-0 (ebook)
[1. Circus—Fiction. 2. Fear—Fiction.] I. Barrager, Brigette, illustrator. II. Title.
III. Title: Louise Trapeze is totally one hundred percent fearless.
PZ7.O8475Lo 2015 [Fic]—dc23 2014021085

MANUFACTURED IN SINGAPORE
10 9 8 7 6 5 4 3 2 1
First Edition

✷ CONTENTS ✷

THE SWEET POTATO POSTER

Boing-flip-boing! I bounced into an extra-high backflip.

In between bounces, I was talking to Stella Dee Saxophone (also known as *my best friend*).

"If *I* were in charge of the official Sweet Potato Traveling Circus Troupe posters, that's what they'd say," I said. "Starring *me*! *Louise Trapeze*! On the flying trapeze! Can you *even*?"

I flipped into another somersault. It might sound

silly that we were having such a serious-business conversation while we bounced all around. But *actually,** we had an excellent reason:

We were practicing our circus tricks on the trampoline!

✸I **LOVE** the word *ACTUALLY.*
It's so grown-up.

It's a good thing Stella and I are best friends. *Best friends* means understanding what someone is saying, even when you're bouncing.

We practice together every morning, after we lead the juggling chickens' *daily constitutional.**

✯ *daily* constitutional= morning exercises that help keep the chickens limber

The chickens' constitutional is just one of our Important Circus Jobs.

We have to get up early each morning to fit everything in. But Stella and I are way too mature to complain.

Being *mature* is a fancy way of saying *grown-up*. And *grown-up* means old enough to fly on the trapeze! I totally, one hundred percent, can't wait until I'm old enough to fly on the trapeze.

According to Mama and Daddy, *old enough* is nine years old. But today I'm only six years and three hundred and sixty-four days old.

And tomorrow, when it's my birthday, I will only be seven. *Not* nine.

I sank on the trampoline and crossed my legs. My face was frowny. "Seven is not grown-up enough to fly! Boo."

Stella made one last *spring-sproing-spring*. She scissored her legs in a side split. Next to us, Clementine the Elephant trumpeted to say the split was perfect. (It was.)

Stella and her parents, Max Saxophone and Ms. Minnie Dee, train and perform with Clementine, and Clementine *loves-loves-loves* Stella. She follows Stella and me everywhere we go.

Stella says it's like having a little sister, except if your sister happens to be a well-trained elephant instead of a human person.

Stella flopped down next to me. "Your backflip is *superb*," she said. *Superb* was one of our new favorite words. (It's much more mature than just plain *super*.)

"Maybe," I said. "Except, in the show, *you* do your splits on top of Clementine way-high-up. I only get to use the solo trapeze. The one that stays still."

FACT: Clementine is even better trained than Stefano Wondrous's Wonder Dogs. And those dogs can count to thirty-seven!

The Easy Trapezees act includes me, Mama, and Daddy. But Mama and Daddy are the only Trapezees who are *actually* allowed to fly from one trapeze bar to another.

"I have to do all of my tricks in *one* place, on *one* bar," I said. "A *Louise-height* bar. It's *so* low down and *so* unmature."

When Stella performs with the Saxophones, she's the Number One Star of the show. She wears a silver leotard and silver ribbons in her hair, and she balances high-high-high on top of Clementine the Elephant *all by herself.* Can you *even*?

It's a good thing I am way too grown-up to be jealous of Stella.

Stella gave me a squishy hug. "Everyone loves your solo tricks, Louise. You'll definitely fly soon."

"Maybe you're right," I said.

"Best friends are *always* right." Stella smiled. "But who cares about flying right now, anyway?" Her eyes twinkled. "Lou, tonight is your Birthday Eve!"

BIRTHDAY EVE

Stella was right. That was an extra-special thing about today:

I wasn't turning nine, but it *was* still my Birthday Eve!

Birthday Eve is one of the very first friendship things Stella and I ever made up. It's when, the night before your birthday, you get to pick what to do. Like if you want to watch a movie, it can be any movie you want, as long as your parents say okay. Or if you want

to play beauty pageant, your best friend has to agree, even if she prefers art projects.

Birthday Eve is *fun-fun-fun.* And this year, I had a super-secret surprise for us.

"I can't believe you still won't tell me the surprise," Stella said.

We were done practicing, and we were heading back to our circus tents. The Sweet Potato tents stretched red-and-yellow swirls all across the Monkey Town fairgrounds.

*Monkey Town** is where we're performing this month. Next we go to *Funky Town**, and then to *Teeny Tiny Town**. After that, we go to *Cleveland.* Then it's back to *Monkey Town* again! We move every month. That's what *traveling circus troupes* do.

✫ Stella and I make up special names for the towns we visit.

? **?** **... BUT** we're still working on a **?** **?** good name for Cleveland. **?**

Stella and I held hands while we walked. Clementine followed right behind. "Look," Stella said. She pointed to the smallest tent, right up front. "Ethel is making her special kettle corn."

Ethel Teitelbaum, our Refreshments Queen, stood by her popcorn cart. Salty-sweet-goodness smells floated our way. Even Clementine made a drooly face.

KETTLE CORN

FACT: Elephants L♥ve kettle corn.

"I hope you girls have time for a tasting later!" Ethel called.

"We will!" Stella and I shouted together.

Tasting the snacks is another one of our Important Circus Jobs. It's one of the most fun jobs of all time ever!

Other Important Circus Jobs we do are:

1. Making sure Dinah-Mite White's cannon is filled up with glitter for when it explodes
2. Oiling Clara Bear's unicycle
3. Brushing the Wonder Dogs' coats

"I have to go try on my new leotard now," Stella said. "But I'll come back after to get ready for Birthday Eve. I can't wait!"

"Me neither!" I waved to Stella and kept walking to the Easy Trapezee tent.

It was extra good that tonight was Birthday Eve. Birthday Eve was exciting.

And *exciting* was the opposite of *maybe-a-teensy-bit-jealous* of Stella's brand-new leotard.

Even without a new leotard of my own, it was still my birthday. Just mine.

And *that* was *totally, one hundred percent,* special!

3

THE THING ABOUT THE CIRCUS

The thing about being in a circus troupe is you have to be brave. Which I totally, one hundred percent, am.

Most of the time.

For instance, like with the rare *arachnids*.*

* **Arachnid** = the grown-up word for spider

I was extremely brave about the rare arachnids. What happened with them was Max Saxophone took Stella and me to the Monkey Town Pet-stravaganza on a day-off Tuesday.

FACT: Day-off Tuesday is every week so the juggling chickens can rest.

We like it there, because they have animals from faraway places. One time, they even had a capuchin monkey!

(That's *actually* why we call it Monkey Town.)

But this time, there were no monkeys. Only creepy-crawly things Stella thought were icky. Stella dared me to peek at the rare arachnid terrarium, *and I did!* I didn't cover my eyes even a smidge. That's how brave I was.

Everyone in the Sweet Potato Circus Troupe is *super* brave. Right next door to my family's tent in our circus village is Leo Torpedo's tent. Leo is a lion, and he leaps through *flaming hoops of fire* in his act! And his partner, Tolstoy the Clown, is brave because he performs with a fierce *lion* (and flaming hoops of fire). Sometimes Tolstoy even puts his head inside Leo's jaws so Leo drools all over his face. The crowd always cheers for that part.

(Crowds like drool.)

Tolstoy and Leo were not being brave right now, though. Leo was hanging out in his cage. Tolstoy was leaning back on a chair, eating a peanut butter sandwich. The peanut butter had rubbed most of his clown lipstick off, so his mouth was just plain mouth-colored now.

Tolstoy waved at me with his non-sandwich hand. "How was trampoline practice?" he asked.

"Bouncy," I said. "Of course."

"Of course," Tolstoy agreed. "A *real* trick would be to invent a trampoline that *didn't* bounce."

I made a face at him. "That wouldn't be a trampoline," I said. "That would just be like the regular ground. Regular ground has already been invented. And also, no one would go to the circus to see it."

Tolstoy nodded. "You may have a point," he said.

I love it when grown-ups say I *may have a point*.

"But, Lou," Tolstoy said, "your mother was looking for you. She's around the back of your tent."

"Thanks!" I said. I ran off lickety-split. Maybe Mama had Birthday Eve news!

Behind the Easy Trapezee tent, Mama was hanging upside down from her aerial hoop. (It's like a trapeze bar, but *actually* a hoop. I have one, too. But mine is Louise-sized, and lower down. *Of course.*)

Even though she was upside down, Mama was having a serious-business conversation with Ringmaster Riley and Daddy. I could tell.

FACT: Mama can do anything upside down. Tie her shoes, eat an orange, brush her teeth... you name it. It's amazing.

You may think a ringmaster is the one person in a circus who *doesn't* have to be brave. But you'd be wrong. Ringmaster Riley is brave for trying to lead "this crazy bunch of loons" (also known as *our troupe*). That's what he always says. Also, his official ringmaster top hat is thirty-six inches tall!

He wasn't wearing his hat right now, though. Now he was whispering to Mama and Daddy. He ran his fingers through his hair so it stood up like porcupine quills. Thinking about Ringmaster Riley with a porcupine on his head made me laugh.

Right when the grown-ups heard me laugh, they stopped whispering. Mama *swoop-swoop-swoop*ed from the hoop to the ground.

"Lou!" Mama said. "You're back early."

"Stella had to try on her new leotard," I said. I tried

not to sound maybe-a-teensy-bit-jealous. But my voice was loudish.

I made my voice as regular as I could. "I'm going to practice tumbling. So that I can be ready to fly," I said. "Even though I'm still not exactly nine, tonight *is* Birthday Eve."

Ringmaster Riley sneaked a *glance** at Mama and Daddy when I said that.

*Glance = a look that means an important secret for grown-ups

Mama smiled wide-wide-wide. *"Actually,* Louise," she said, "we've got a special Birthday Eve surprise for you."

Daddy picked up a giant box tied with a fat gold bow and handed it to me. I popped it open, fast as I could.

I gasped. *"Cheeze Louise and holy trapeze!"**

CHEEZE LOUISE AND HOLY TRAPEZE! is my special catchphrase. That's an expression that's one hundred percent Louise. If you want a catchphrase of your very own, you'll have to make it up yourself.

"It's a brand-new costume for your *debut* on the flying trapeze!" Mama said.

Debut is a fancy way of saying *first time ever*. And my new costume was *fancy*!

It was a magenta leotard. (*Magenta* is a bright pinkish-purple color.) It had a tulle tutu skirt in magenta and silver ruffles, too, and there were matching sequined tights and also a ruffled headband that would be perfect for holding back my crazy-twisty-noodle curls.

My tutu was maybe even a *smidge* fancier than Stella's new leotard, *actually*. Even though I was too mature to say so.

"Lady Edwina designed that, just for you," Ringmaster Riley said. Lady Edwina is our Costume Director. That means she's the boss of what we wear in our show.

I looked at Mama and Daddy. "Does this mean what I think it does?"

Mama smooched me on the top of my head. "Happy Birthday Eve, Louise," she said. "Are you ready to fly?"

TALLER THAN AN ELEPHANT

Mama, Daddy, and Ringmaster Riley were making giant happy-for-me faces.

"Your solo routine is in tip-top shape," Mama said. "And your hip circles and knee hangs are *superb*." Mama grinned because she'd used one of my new favorite words.

"So what if you did one of your best tricks—but on the flying trapeze instead of your solo bar?" Daddy asked. "You could swing out and do a split. It's not a new trick, but it would still be more *mature* to be higher up, right?"

"Right!" I said. What an excellent plan!

"You can just drop to the net after," Daddy said. "Like on the trampoline, but more dramatic."

"Hooray!" I shouted. This plan was getting better and better.

Then I looked at the mature-person-sized flying trapeze rig. It was tall. *Much* taller than my solo trapeze.

The trapeze net was made of thick, knotty white rope. And the platform to the trapeze bar was *high-high-high* up in the air.

Mama and Daddy climbed up to that platform every time we performed. But now that it was my turn, those ladders looked tall as giants.

Actually, now that I looked again, the trapeze really was *extremely* tall. Taller than Clementine the Elephant even.

Also, the ropes of the net were woven very wide and loose-ish. Mama and Daddy were too big to slip through the holes. But I was much smaller than them.

Maybe I was even *so* small that I'd—*swish-swoosh-slam*—slide right through the ropes and land smack on the ground on my *keister*!*

*Keister = what Lady Edwina calls your tush. Cady the Bearded Lady's keister is so big she has to wear giant-sized overalls. But people don't notice her keister—they're too busy looking at her beard!

My heart did a *skitter-skitter-skitter*. Landing on your keister in the middle of a circus performance is not grown-up at all.

Ringmaster Riley cleared his throat. In his most

announcer-ish voice, he said, *"Ladies and gentlemen! Feast your eyes on the fabulous flying debut of Sweet Potato's own LOUISE TRAPEZE!"*

I looked at Mama and Daddy. They were smiling so hard their eyes were squished up. I tried to squish-smile back at them, but my eyes didn't want to go.

The trapeze. It was so extra high!

And the net. It was so extra wide!

I opened my mouth. "I think . . ."

But then I stopped. Everyone looked so happy for me. How could I tell them what I was feeling?

What if they thought I was being babyish?

Eureka! I thought. (That's the noise your brain makes when a good idea pops into it.) I knew what to say.

"I should wait for Stella," I told them. "Important times are for best friends."

"Hmm. You have a point," Mama said. "Of course

you can wait for Stella. For now, we'll raise your tightwire so you can practice. A higher wire *and* the flying trapeze would make a great birthday show!"

"Totally," I agreed. But my voice was quiet-ish. I barely cared that Mama said I *had a point.* I was just glad I didn't have to climb the extra-high trapeze ladder yet. I wanted to fly *so* much. But the truth was, I realized I also had a deepest, darkest secret:

I, Louise Trapeze, am totally, one hundred percent, afraid of heights!

5

NINETY-EIGHT PERCENT FEARLESS

Totally, one hundred percent, fearless means *not afraid of anything.*

Not even heights or wide nets.

It did not matter that I had bravely peeked at a rare arachnid. I was not one hundred percent fearless. More like ninety-eight percent.

Which was a lot percent for a six-year-old. But tomorrow was my birthday. And on my birthday, I was *going to fly.*

I was all alone with Mama's aerial hoop, my teensy-bit-higher wire, and that gigantic, *extra-dramatic* flying trapeze.

I looked at the trapeze.

I looked at its platform.

I looked at its ladder.

They were all still gigantic. And *very* high up in the air.

Maybe I'd start with my higher wire that Mama and Daddy had raised. It was much lower to the ground than an elephant. You climb a big-time ladder to get to the platform of a *high wire*. But mine was so low I just used a special Louise-sized ladder. The low wire was usually about at my waist. Now that it was a teensy bit higher up—not quite at my shoulder—it was still fine for the Louise ladder. So it couldn't be scary.

Could it?

Step.

Step.

Step.

   Breathe.

   Breathe.

   Breathe.

It didn't take long to get to the top of the Louise ladder. But once I did, it still felt pretty high up. The tightwire looked skinny and slippery, and it didn't have a net at all.

Not even the wide, knotty, fall-on-your-keister kind.

I wasn't feeling less afraid of heights. I was feeling worse! I wished I'd never asked to fly on the trapeze in the first place.

"Nice tightwire!" I heard from nearby. "At least you finally got it off the ground. *Barely.*"

There was a snicker.

A *ferrety* snicker.

It was Fernando Worther.

Also known as: *Ferret-breath Fernando.*

My big-time enemy.

FERRET-BREATH FERNANDO

Fernando Worther is totally my big-time enemy. He's the only gooberhead in our entire troupe. Everyone else in our circus family is nice.

Fernando is Ringmaster Riley's son. He thinks he's hot tamale sauce because he's nine. Stella and I call him *Ferret-breath*. That's because Fernando has a pet ferret named Linus who *sleeps in Fernando's bed with him*! Can you *even*?

Yuck.

FACT: Linus is **NOT** a circus ferret, just the regular kind. He doesn't know any tricks. And he's EXTRA smelly. Even for a ferret.

"You're a real daredevil, Louise," Fernando said. "On Planet Opposite." He laughed at his own joke like it was *actually* funny. (It was not.)

Fernando is the stilt walker in our circus. He wears his stilts everywhere. That meant he was much higher up than I was, even standing on my Louise ladder. I had to tilt back just to see his whole gooberhead at once.

"If it's so easy, why don't *you* try it?" I stuck my tongue out, even though it was a babyish thing to do. Fernando wouldn't try the tightwire. He would never, ever take off his stilts.

"Thanks, but I've got an act that doesn't need training wheels," he said. He swayed *close-close-close* to me, just to show off how good he was.

"Well, of course you're superb at stilts. It's the only thing you do," I snapped. "It's different when you have to learn a whole *aerial arts repertoire.*"*

*Reportoire= a French way of saying different tricks that make up a big routine, not just one plain old talent (like STILTS)

Fernando smirked. "*Actually,* stilts *aren't* that easy," he said. "*For instance,* they wouldn't be easy to learn at all . . . if you were *afraid of heights.*"

My face got very hot. Fernando had guessed my deepest, darkest secret!

"Well, *I'm* not afraid of heights. Not even a teensy percent," I said.

"Okay," Fernando replied. But he shrugged like he didn't believe me.

"You'll see," I said. My voice was a little bit shouty again. "You think you're so great because you're nine. But tomorrow is my Actual Birthday Day, and it's going to be my *fabulous flying debut*! Just wait!"

"Louise?" said a friendly voice from the tent behind me.

I heard the thumping of elephant footsteps. Stella and Clementine! Stella was still wearing her brand-new leotard.

Actually, it looked extremely perfect on her.

Everything always looks extremely perfect on Stella. And even if she's afraid of rare arachnids, she is not afraid of heights one bit. *Pfft.* *

*PFFT= my most grouchy noise

Stella didn't notice how grumpy I was. "Your parents are letting you fly for your birthday?" she called. Her leotard was glimmery in the sunshine. "Wow!"

"They totally are!" I said. "Even if *this* gooberhead doesn't believe me."

"Ignore him," Stella said. "Your tightwire is higher up, too! Superb!" She was best-friend-forever excited for me. *BFF* excited! That made me cheerier.

"Come down! Show me what you're going to do for your trapeze act!" she called.

Fernando laughed.

"Yeah, Louise," he said. "If you're not afraid of heights, why don't you show us?"

7

TIME TO FLY

Fernando and Stella were waiting for me.

And *then* they were waiting for me to swing on the flying trapeze.

"I *will* show you!" I said. I tried to sound brave. I climbed back down the tightwire ladder without wobbling once.

But then it was time for the flying trapeze. The *way-high-up* flying trapeze.

I took a deep, being-fearless breath and forced

myself to walk to the trapeze, even though my hands were getting very shake-ish and sweaty.

Step.

Step.

Step.

Now I was in front of the ladder. I grabbed it with both hands. It felt slippery because of my sweaty palms.

FACT: Trapeze artists put chalk on their palms to keep them unsweaty. But the chalk bag for our trapeze was on the platform at the top of the ladder. So that was no help at all.

I wiped my palms on my pants and grabbed the ladder again. I stepped up.

Breathe.

Breathe.

Breathe.

I lifted one foot on top of the other, rung to rung.

Climb.

Climb.

Climb.

After what felt like *foreverness,* I was at the top. I stepped onto the platform. One trapeze bar swayed in front of me. It was too far away to grab.

I looked down at Fernando and Stella. "I can't reach the bar," I called. Maybe I wouldn't have to fly for them after all.

Fernando snickered. But Stella made an asking face at Clementine. Clementine nodded and stomped over to the trapeze. She wrapped her trunk around me.

"Clem's going to help you!" Stella shouted.

"Oh, good," I said. But my voice was small. *Actually,* I didn't think it was so good at all.

Actually, my head was going to maybe tell my stomach to throw up *any minute now.*

I squeezed my eyes shut. When I opened them again, Clem had moved me gently to the bar and let me go.

I wrapped my hands around it *tight-tight-tight.* Clementine blinked at me. She gave me a tiny push with her trunk.

Swing.

Swing.

Swing.

"Do a split, Lou!" Stella called.

(I am *superb* at splits on my plain old Louise-sized solo trapeze.)

This is exactly the same, I told myself.

But deep down, it didn't *feel* exactly the same.

"She can't!" Ferret-breath said.

That made me the angriest. I do *not* like when

ferrety boys tell me I can't do things. "Yes," I shouted,
"I CAN!"

It was time to fly.

"Cheeze Louise and holy TRAPEZE!"

I glued my legs together and pointed my toes. I
pulled in all my muscles, then swung my legs *forward-
backward-forward*, and *swoop-swoop-swoop*ed my
right leg up and under the bar. I arched my back.

Flip-flop-flip!

I had turned totally upside down, my hands still grabbing the bar and my legs in a perfect split! I did it!

I DID IT!

I did a split on the flying trapeze!

From the ground, Stella clapped and cheered. Clementine stomped her feet (it's the elephant way of clapping). Petrova the Human Pretzel was there now, too, all twisted up pretzel-y, applauding. I felt *proud-proud-proud*.

Until all of a sudden, my big moment wasn't so proud-making anymore.

Instead, it had changed into something else: an *Extremely Embarrassing Time. . . .*

8

EXTREMELY EMBARRASSING

My split was all finished. I was hanging again. More and more Sweet Potatoes were arriving to see my Extremely Embarrassing Time! Everyone was looking up at me, waiting. My arms were achy.

It was time to drop to the net.

The wide, knotty net that was *very* far away.

My brain said: *The net is safety.*

My feelings said: *Nuh-uh.*

If I couldn't drop down to the net, what would

happen? Would I just stay there, way-high-up, *forever*?

That sounded like a terrible plan. And the embarrassing feeling was *not* getting better.

"Are you okay, Lou?" Stella called.

"I'm *superb*!" I said. But really, I felt silly. And a *smidge* grumpy again. I was going to be swinging from this trapeze bar for the rest of my lifelong days.

"Come down and try another trick!" That was Maharaja Moe, the snake charmer. Khan, his ten-foot cobra, was curled around Maharaja's neck.

I thought I might faint.

But fainting would mean falling

down to the net, and I *definitely* wasn't going to do that.

I couldn't faint, I couldn't drop, and I for certainly couldn't sway there for the rest of my life. What *could* I do?

"Actually," I called, "instead of doing more tricks, I'm going to *take it easy.** So I'll be rested for my fabulous Actual Birthday Day debut!"

*Take it easy = grown-up for RELAX AND EAT SOME FRESH-MADE KETTLE CORN

Maharaja and the others nodded like that made sense. But I was still stuck, hanging from the trapeze bar. That was definitely still a problem.

Stella looked up at me. Then she and Fernando made a little *glance* at each other.

I did *not* like my BFF glancing at Ferret-breath.

But all Stella said to me was "Good idea." She turned to Clementine. "Since Louise wants to take it easy, can you help her back down?"

"*Excellent* thinking, Stella," I said.

It *was* excellent thinking.

Even if it maybe meant she and Fernando *both* guessed my deepest, darkest secret.

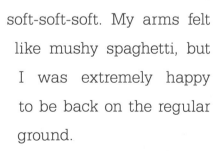

Clementine wrapped me in her trunk again and lowered me down, soft-soft-soft. My arms felt like mushy spaghetti, but I was extremely happy to be back on the regular ground.

"Hooray!" cheered Maharaja. Petrova whistled. Khan flicked his tongue.

Stella and Fernando didn't cheer, though. They were still making little glances at each other.

My stomach squeezed up when they did that. I was still afraid of heights. Ferret-breath Fernando knew it. Stella probably knew it. And tomorrow, everyone else would know it, too.

It was too hard to be mature and not jealous of Stella right now! "Thanks for getting Clem to help me," I said to her. "But I have to go . . . get the surprise ready for Birthday Eve."

"Of course," Stella said. "Birthday Eve. It will be so, so fun."

"It will," I agreed.

But neither of us was smiling.

9

SCAREDNESS THINGS

Birthday Eve *was* fun.

It was late-late-late. Stella and I were having our sleepover. We'd stretched out sleeping bags in the Easy Trapezee tent *all by ourselves.* (Mama and Daddy were sleeping in our *trailer,** right in front of the tent.)

*A trailer is a little house that's also a bus. Our troupe travels in trailers. Also, that's where we sleep.

(Except, not Stella and me on Birthday Eve Night.)

"Do you want another watermelon gummy?" Stella asked.

"No thanks. I'm full," I answered. "Maybe just one more glitter tattoo instead."

We still had lots of tattoos left over from Mama's present. That was the super-secret Birthday Eve surprise: a *Deluxe Glitter Tattoo Kit* from the Funky Town Odditorium Emporium! Mama saw it in the store and knew it would be perfect for Stella and me. And she was right!

"How about this one? It's a butterfly," Stella said.

"Yes, please." There was one teensy section of my right hand still untattooed, next to my thumb. I held my hand out. Stella reached over and stuck the tattoo on. She patted it with a wet sponge. Then she peeled the backing off.

"That looks perfect," I said.

I blew on my hand until I was sure my tattoo was dry. Then I unzipped my sleeping bag and snuggled inside. The butterfly tattoo really did look *superb*. It made me feel better about my Extremely Embarrassing Time up on the trapeze.

Stella snuggled into her sleeping bag, too. She yawned. "Did we take it easy enough for your fabulous *debut*?" she asked.

We hadn't talked about my flying. Or the Embarrassing Time. Or the not-smiling-at-each-other from before.

"Of course!" I said. I tried to sound extra cheery. But I remembered how Stella *glanced* at Fernando.

Then Stella said, "Lou?"

My heart made a *thump-thump-thump*. Stella

sounded like she had a serious-business question. But I just said, "Mm-hm?" like I wasn't so worried.

"You know that I'm scared of lots of things," Stella said.

"I know." It was true. I counted Stella's Scaredness Things on my fingers. "Monsters, masks, staying inside the car for the car wash, and also the moon."

Some of the things on Stella's list were a little silly. But I never teased her about them. Teasing is not a best friend way to be.

"And you are scared of yapper dogs," Stella said.

"I *do not care for them*. Because of their yappy barks," I explained. It wasn't *exactly* a fear, but yappy barks make my nose go wrinkly.

"You *do not care for them*," Stella agreed. "But . . . if you had *another* Scaredness

Thing to add to your list, that would be okay. Like if you were scared of zombie movies. Or centipedes. Or even . . . high-up places?"

My heart *thump*ed again. My best friend *did* guess my deepest, darkest secret! What if she and Fernando even *joked about my scaredness together, behind my back*?!

I didn't think my BFF would do that to me. But I wasn't for-totally certain. After all, Stella was extremely perfect at everything she did. And Fernando was *superb* on his stilts.

Maybe they were so-so-*so* much more mature than me that now . . .

they were going to be . . .

BFFs . . .

with each other?!

FACT: That was the VERY mosT WORST thought I'd had in my whole, entire lifelong time.

It was a horrible feeling. Like there was a giant glob of peanut butter stuck in my throat, and I couldn't talk around it.

I coughed and tried to push the lump down. "I need to be totally, one hundred percent, fearless," I said. "To be *mature.*"

"Louise, one hundred percent is *all* the percents!" Stella said. "You could still be ninety-nine percent fearless! Or even ninety-eight percent! That's *a lot* percent!"

I liked that Stella felt the *exact same way* about ninety-eight percent as I did. It *was* a lot percent. But it wasn't one hundred.

My grumpiness was back, big-time. "That's easy for *you* to say," I said. "You're *already* the star of your act. You're not afraid of standing way-high-up on Clementine's back at all!"

Stella blinked at me. "But I'm not one hundred

percent fearless! Or even ninety-eight percent! My Scaredness List is *so long!*"

Stella's Scaredness List:
- monsters
- masks
- the car wash
- the MOON

Suddenly, words started pushing *fast-fast-fast* out of my mouth, before my brain could think them all the way through. "But it doesn't matter for you, because you *always* do everything *extremely perfectly!*"

I couldn't stop the words from rushing out. "Fernando thinks I can't fly because I'm afraid of heights. And you do, too! You were probably talking all about it *together, behind my back*!"

Stella gulped. Her eyes were teary. "Why would I be talking to *Ferret-breath* about you?" she asked. "You're my BFF, Lou."

"Maybe," I grumped. "But if you and Fernando are so busy *glancing* at each other, maybe you don't need me for a BFF anymore." Now my eyes were teary, too. This was a terrible Birthday Eve.

"Well, if you're going to be so mean, maybe I *don't*," Stella said.

"Fine!" I folded my arms. "If you don't need me, you don't have to stay here. Birthday Eve sleepovers are only for best friends."

I hoped she wouldn't *actually* leave.

Stella wiped her eyes. "Of course I'm staying," she said. "I don't want to fight. And I *don't* have any secrets with Fernando."

"Great," I said. "And *I* don't have any new Scared-ness Things to add to my list."

"Great!" Stella said. "Happy Birthday Eve. Good night."

"Good night," I said back.

But on the inside, I wasn't feeling so good at all.

BAD-MOOD FEELINGS

Mama says that sometimes bad-mood feelings go away after a good night's sleep. So when I woke up on Actual Birthday Day, the first thing I did was lie super still to see what my mood was. I thought maybe being seven years old now would help me feel better.

FACT: My stomach was ACTUALLY squeezier than ever.

It was a terrible way to feel on Actual Birthday Day.

But when I sat up, I saw something that made me smile wide-wide-wide:

My beautiful, *unique-and-special-just-for-ME* magenta leotard with the ruffled tutu was right there, waiting!

Mama must have sneaked it in while we were sleeping. It was hanging from a rolling clothing rack. There was a card taped to the front of the leotard, too. I got up and ran to it, lickety-split. I ripped the envelope open and pulled out the card.

Congratulations to our darling Louise!

Happy Actual Birthday Day! ♥

Take this costume to Lady Edwina's tent today at 9 a.m. for a final fitting. We can't wait to see you FLY!

x's and o's
Mama & Daddy

⭐x's and o's are hugs and kisses when you write them in a card. Other times, they're just regular letters.

My stomach squeezed straight up into my throat. My beautiful costume was a birthday present. And now Mama and Daddy expected me to fly.

I *definitely* couldn't tell anyone about my fear of heights.

But I *totally* couldn't fly on the trapeze! Not after what happened yesterday.

I probably wouldn't even be able to wear my new costume with its ruffly tutu and headband! And that costume was basically the top-most-amazing birthday present ever.

It was all just the very saddest. I didn't know what to do.

And then: *Eureka!*

I had a Very Brilliant Idea.

I was supposed to wear my costume for my *fabulous flying debut.*

But if I didn't *have* a new costume to wear . . .

Maybe my fabulous debut would have to wait!

Stella was still snoring. It was early-early-early. I quickly changed out of my pajamas into regular clothes. Then I pulled the costume off the rack and crept outside. The circus tents and trailers were very still. That was good. Because I needed to find a place to hide my costume before anyone else woke up.

Thank goodness I was so full of Very Brilliant Ideas. Because just then, I remembered a *magnificent secret:*

The Trick of the Aztec Tomb.

11

THE TRICK OF THE AZTEC TOMB

In our circus troupe, we have a magician. His name is Magnificent Blue.

Magnificent Blue knows lots of *stupendous* feats of magic. For instance, he can saw his assistant, Miss Kitty Fantastico, right *in half*!

(He puts her back together after, good as new.)

But my number one favorite of Blue's tricks is:

How it works is: Miss Kitty Fantastico rolls the tomb out to the center ring so the crowd can see how huge it is. It's eight whole feet tall!

Miss Kitty shows the audience how the silky salmon-pink lining of the tomb is sewed up tight-tight-tight. Magnificent Blue takes off his *fancy magician's topcoat*. (This is so everyone sees there's nothing "up his sleeves.")

Then Miss Kitty *locks him in the tomb and turns it around three times*!

After the audience says the magic words—

"Abracadabra, banana SPLITSVILLE!"—there's a *huge* flash of light and a *kaboom!* Miss Kitty unlocks the door to the tomb and opens it all-the-way-wide.

Each time: *Magnificent Blue is GONE! Poof,* he has escaped!

The audience *always* gasps.

The trick is *amazing.*

And *I,* Louise Trapeze, *know how it works.*

Magnificent Blue taught me once, as a *thank-you* for helping him sort his magic scarves. It's *actually* very simple. Inside the lining of the tomb is a tiny *hidden latch.* When that latch is unhooked, Magnificent Blue sneaks through a trapdoor to a secret compartment underneath! That's how he disappears.

So, that is the thing I know about the Aztec Tomb. And here is *another* thing I knew that morning:

Magnificent Blue wasn't performing that week. He was away at a special Magic Camp for Professional

Grown-Up Magicians. He was going to catch up with our troupe back in Funky Town.

That meant the Aztec Tomb was just sitting in our prop trailer, all alone.

And *that* meant the Aztec Tomb would be the absolute *perfect* place to hide my brand-new birthday costume!

It was the greatest *eureka!* plan ever!

The prop trailer was stuffed to the gills with crates and cages and old light-up signs. There was even a giant wire basket filled with Tolstoy's squeaking red rubber noses.

FACT: Tolstoy buys his red squeaker noses in bulk from the Internet.

And then: there it was!

The Aztec Tomb!

I rushed to it. The tomb door opened with a squeak, and I grabbed the lining, feeling for the latch.

I got it!

The super-secret door swung toward me. *Scrunch-scrunch-scrunch.* I wadded my leotard, my tights, and even my beautiful headband into the *teensiest* ball it could be. Then I stuffed everything into the secret compartment.

I felt sad seeing my special costume smushed up on the floor of the tomb. And I felt sad thinking I was going to miss my fabulous *debut*.

But I decided being afraid of heights was worse than being sad. So I closed the tomb back up and tiptoed outside.

The sky was bluer now, and people and animals and all kinds of Sweet Potatoes were moving around. But no one had seen me come out of the prop trailer, thank goodness gracious.

"Louise! There you are!" It was Stella. "I woke up and you were gone! Where'd you go?" She gave me a for-serious look. "Are you still upset about our fight? I feel bad about it."

"Me too," I said. "I shouldn't have been so mean about Fernando. I know you'd never take a goober-head's side over mine."

"Never," Stella agreed.

I didn't know what to say to Stella about what I *had* been doing, though. I for certainly couldn't tell her about hiding my costume.

But before I could say anything, Stella grabbed me. She pulled me toward the Big Top. "If we're not in a fight anymore, you have to come with me right now!" she said.

"What's going on?" I asked.

"You'll see!" Stella promised. "Close your eyes."

12

A SWEET POTATO SURPRISE

I squeezed my eyes shut. I let Stella guide me into the Big Top tent.

And *then*! The most unexpected thing of *ever* happened!

"Surprise!" Lots of voices shouted at me in a happy way.

I was so startled! But it was a good kind of startled. Because the entire Sweet Potato Troupe was gathered under the Big Top *just for me*! In the middle of the tent was a shiny rainbow-colored sign.

"It's a Happy Birthday Breakfast," Stella explained.

I looked around. There was a folding table set up with breakfasty muffins, and doughnuts with sprinkles *and* chocolate chips, and a large pot of coffee for the grown-ups to drink. The Wonder Dogs were playing "Happy Birthday" music on their red plastic doggie pianos. And the juggling chickens were juggling yellow-frosted cupcakes up-up-up into the air without even getting any frosting on their feathers.

"Don't worry," Stella whispered. "We have different cupcakes for eating."

That was good news.

FACT: Yellow frosting is the best kind.

I laughed with Stella and hugged Mama and Daddy. Clara Bear unicycled up and popped a sparkly tiara on my head. Then there was singing. Even the chickens clucked along.

"We're so excited for you, Lou," said Petrova. "Fernando told us you're going to be the star of the flying trapeze tonight!"

Ferret-breath. Why did he have to be such a gooberhead all the time? Suddenly he was right there, staring at me with ferrety eyes.

"That's what you said, right?" he asked.

"Of course!" I said. "I'm going to fly."

"She's going to do a split on the flying trapeze," Stella said. "And her tightwire is higher up now, too."

"Oh, can we get a sneak peek?" Cady the Bearded Lady asked.

"Do a turn on the tightwire, Lou!" cried Stefano Wonder.

Everyone was looking at me and cheering me on. I was sorry I'd said anything to Fernando about flying. I was sorry I'd said anything to *anyone* about flying.

"I can't," I said in a quiet-mouse voice. But no one could hear me over the cheering.

"Lou! Lou! Lou!" They were so loud!

I took a deep breath.

"I CAN'T!" I said. My voice came out extra shouty.

Mama wrinkled her forehead. "What do you mean?"

My eyes got watery. It was time for the hardest part of the *eureka!* plan. Now I had to tell a *little white lie.**

✤Little white Lie = A small fib that doesn't _ACTUALLY_ hurt anyone. But even white lies can make your throat feel peanut-butter-lumpy.

"I can't go on the flying trapeze tonight," I said.

"Why not?" Daddy asked gently.

"Because . . ." I swallowed hard. "My costume is missing."

SCAREDY-SNAKE

Everyone gasped. Ringmaster Riley waved his arms. In his biggest announcer voice, he said, *"We* must *find Louise's costume!"*

"Don't you worry," he said to me. "We'll all search high and low. We'll find your costume!"

"Indeed!" shouted Lady Edwina.

FACT: ACTUALLY, that was exactly what I was afraid of.

Maharaja Moe stepped forward. "Khan will look underneath our equipment, and in the corners of the tents and the trailers," he said. "Cobras are good at slithering into tight spaces."

I was worried. What if *tight spaces* meant the secret compartment of the Aztec Tomb? Khan wriggled away in a flash. I had to stop him!

But before I could quick-think of how, Miss Kitty joined in. "I can check all the magic props," she said. "In Blue's things, it would be easy for something to—*poof!*—vanish."

"No!" I blurted.* "You can't!"

*✶ BLURTeD = called out or interrupted in a nervous way

Everyone looked at me. I had to think of something unblurty to say.

"It's just, the prop trailer is so big! You can't search it alone. I'll help!" I offered.

"Great!" Miss Kitty said. "Between you, me, and Khan, we'll find *some* kind of clue!"

I for sure hope not, I thought, walking away very quickly. I was nearly out of earshot when Daddy called me back.

"Lou," he asked, with his thinking face on, "is there something you want to tell us?"

I looked at Daddy and Mama.

They looked right back at me.

"No," I said. "Of course not."

Before they could ask me anything else, I ran off again.

And I didn't look back at them once.

Right away at the prop trailer, I noticed three important things:

1. The door to the trailer was open just a teensy bit. *For instance,* the amount a cobra might need to sneak inside!

2. One of the trailer windows was open, too!! Just the perfect amount for a cobra to slither through!!

3. Khan the Cobra had already gone inside— probably through the door—and come out again—probably through the window—*with my costume*!!!

Then he *took my costume way-high-up into the tallest tree around*!!!!

And the reason I knew that Khan had slithered my

costume into the tall-tall-tall tree
was:

The costume was up there! Stuck in the branches!

And there was Khan, a few branches below, slithering around and around and around. He looked as sad as a cobra could look.

"The costume is stuck!" Miss Kitty Fantastico shouted when she saw me. "Khan already found it in the trailer! He brought it out the window and into the tree, but now he can't get it loose."

"Of course not!" Fernando said. "Snakes don't have hands." He laughed.

"This is no time for jokes!" I shouted. Poor Khan looked so upset. "He must have found it in the false bottom of the Aztec Tomb! But why didn't he just go back out the door, like he came in?"

"I don't know," Maharaja said. "But it's a problem. Because even though Khan can slither underneath, up, and around things, he's not great at slithering *back down* from high places. We've been working on it." Maharaja made a whisper-voice, like he didn't want Khan to hear what he said next. *"I think he is afraid of heights."*

Oh no! If anyone understood how awful it was to be afraid of heights, it was me.

This was all my fault.

"Hey," Fernando said suddenly. "You said Khan got the costume from the Aztec Tomb. How did you *know* the costume was in there, Louise?"

I froze up. "I just . . . guessed," I said. "It sounded like a place a missing costume could be."

I could tell Fernando didn't believe me.

Next to Fernando, Mama and Daddy had their thinking faces on again. It was very quiet. I knew that, really and truly, it was time to be one hundred percent honest. But I didn't know where to begin.

And then, the most babyish thing of all time happened.

I started to cry!

14

A SECRET OF GROWN-UPS

There I was, crying in front of *everyone*! It was my second Extremely Embarrassing Time since my birthday began. Gently, Mama took my hand.

"Let's talk, Louise," she said. She led me around the back of the Big Top tent so we could be just-us-alone.

We sat crisscross on a grassy patch next to a big crate of confetti and a box of squishy juggling balls.

"So, Louise." Mama's voice was very parent-ish.

"Everyone in the troupe spent their valuable time looking for *your* costume."

I swallowed. It made me feel terrible to think about that.

"And now Khan is stuck in a tree. Maharaja says he's very scared. Can you imagine how he feels?" Mama looked at me with laser-beam eyes, like she

knew down-deep-on-the-inside that *actually,* I knew *exactly* what that was like.

"Why *did* you mention the Aztec Tomb, Lou?" Mama asked.

All the feelings squeezing in my stomach finally squeezed their way out.

"Because it was me!" I said. "I hid the costume in the Aztec Tomb!"

Mama put her hands on my shoulders. "What's going on, Louise? Why did you do that?" she asked.

I sniffled. Her hands felt warm in a good, Mama-ish way. But I was still too embarrassed to tell her my secret.

But then Mama surprised me! "Does this have any-thing to do with your new starring role in our circus act?" she asked.

I looked at her. "How did you guess?"

Mama smiled. "Mother's Intuition."*

★Mother's Intuition = a Mama thing of always knowing the truth about my inside thoughts. It's like a magic power!

It was time to share my secret Scaredness Thing with someone. And since Mama had such amazing intuition, she'd probably understand.

I took a *giant* being-fearless breath. And this time, it worked! I looked straight at Mama and said, "The flying trapeze is so way-high-up! I tried, but I couldn't drop to the net. It was too, too scary."

And then, in my quietest tiny-mouse voice, I told Mama the totally, one hundred percent, truth:

"I think I am afraid of heights."

There.

It was out.

My deepest, darkest secret was not a secret anymore.

I waited for Mama to yell or shout, or tell me I had to leave the Sweet Potato Circus forever because of being so unmature.

But instead, Mama did the strangest thing ever:

She *laughed*!

"This isn't funny!" I said. "If I'm only ninety-eight percent fearless, then I'm not brave enough to be in our circus! What if Ringmaster Riley makes me *leave*?"

Mama made a funny face. "No one's going to make you leave the troupe. You're an Easy Trapezee, Louise!"

I sighed. What a relief!

"That's really what you're worried about?" Mama asked. "That being afraid of heights makes you less grown-up?"

I nodded.

Mama smooched me on the top of my head. "Well, I have a little secret for you about grown-ups."

My eyes went wide-wide-wide.

FACT: Grown-up secrets are my *favorite*.

"Grown-ups are afraid of things, too. It's normal. It *doesn't* make you less mature. *Actually*"—she smiled—"being able to talk about the things you're afraid of makes you *extra* grown-up. That's how you learn to face your fears. Besides, if you're not afraid, you don't get to be brave."

Hmm.

It *was* true that since being honest with Mama, I was feeling much better already.

"You have excellent Mother's Intuition," I said.

Mama hugged me. "If you're not ready to fly, that's fine," she said. "You'll be ready before you know it. Until then, there are lots of special lower-down tricks we can add to your act to make it jazzier. Even in time for tonight," she said. "Your birthday performance *is* going to be unique, I promise."

Lower-down tricks sounded great. *Jazzier* sounded even better. "So I can wear the new leotard?" I asked in my most hopeful voice.

"As soon as we can get it—and Khan—down from that tree!" Mama said.

"Actually," I told her, "I may have a fantastic *eureka!* plan about that."

15

THE EUREKA! PLAN

Quick-quick-quick, I ran back to the way-high-up tall tree. Everyone had gathered while I was talking with Mama. Khan was still all wound up in the branches.

Clementine was standing next to Stella, like always. I ran up and patted her on her wrinkly elephant side. When she looked at me, I pointed at her trunk, then into the tree, and finally at myself. Clementine

blinked at me with her big, round elephant eyes. I knew she understood.

"Cheeze Louise and holy trapeze!" I whispered to myself. It was time to be totally brave.

Clem reached out and wrapped her trunk around me. *Whoosh-whoosh-whoosh!* She lifted me up toward the tree. Quickly, I untangled my costume from the branch it was caught on. Then Clementine lowered me level with Khan.

I leaned over and whispered in my softest, most Mama-ish voice. "I know it's scary way-high-up," I told him. "But I'm here, and so is Clem. We've got you. It's safe."

And even though I was still *approximately**** two percent afraid of heights myself, I meant it. Even way-high-up, I was safe. And Khan would be, too.

☆*Approximately* = grown-up word for *just about*

I stretched out my hand. Slowly, Khan slithered over to me, winding around my arm. Clementine carefully lowered us both to the ground.

Once we were safely down, Khan gave me a flickery cobra kiss on my nose. He wriggled back to Maharaja. Everyone cheered like crazy.

Lady Edwina grabbed my costume from me. "Let me see if it needs any last-minute repairs," she said. "It's not supposed to get tangled in trees!"

"It's my fault," I said. "I hid it in the Aztec Tomb." It was easier to talk about since I'd told Mama the truth. "I was afraid to go way-high-up on the flying trapeze. But Mama says if I'm not ready, I don't have to make my debut tonight. I still get to wear my costume, though!"

"Of course you do!" Lady Edwina said. "It's your birthday!"

"But, Lou," Stella cut in, "you might be more ready to fly than you think."

Easy for Stella to say, I thought.

"I'm not," I told her. "I'm afraid of heights. I didn't want to tell you. That's why I was so grumpy at our sleepover last night."

Being honest didn't make all the jealous feelings go away, but it felt good to tell the truth to my BFF anyway.

Stella smiled. "I forgive you for being grumpy. Birthday Eve means you can be in any mood you want."

FACT: Being BFFs with Stella is the best-best-best!

"So you *actually can* add another Scaredness Thing to my list," I admitted.

"I don't care about your List of Scaredness Things," Stella said. "You just let Clementine lift you *way-high-up* into the air—the same way she helped you down from the trapeze yesterday!" She grabbed my shoulders. "You didn't even think twice! All you needed was Clem's help. How brave is *that*?"

"*Extremely* brave, I'd say," Daddy chimed in.

My heart did a flutter. Was Stella right? Was I *actually* brave . . . with a little help from my best circus friends?

Actually, I *totally* was!

I felt warm and friendship-fuzzy. But then I thought of something. "Clementine isn't an Easy Trapezee. She's part of *your* act. Not mine," I said.

"Don't be silly." Stella glanced at Clementine. "We can make an Official Birthday Exception."

Clementine trumpeted to say she agreed, and Max Saxophone and Ms. Minnie Dee nodded their heads, too.

FACT: BFFs means sharing elephant friends, especially for Official Birthday Exceptions.

"Louise and Clementine know a *superb* trick," Stella told Mama and Daddy.

"We do!" I said. "Instead of falling to the net after I do my trapeze trick, Clementine carries me down to the ground. We practiced it yesterday."

"You *have* to do that trick in your act tonight!" Stella said.

I turned to Mama and Daddy. "Can I? Prettiest please with a lemon drop?"

"How can we say no to such a mature, talented birthday girl?" Daddy replied.

"You're definitely ready for your fabulous debut, Louise," Mama said.

"Definitely, completely, and totally!" I did a happy twirl. "I'm *at least* ninety-nine percent ready now."

Daddy laughed. "Ninety-nine percent is plenty."

"I agree!" I said.

This was the cheeriest birthday ever. I couldn't wait to put on my new costume and be the Number One Special Star of the Easy Trapezees' show. And I couldn't wait to have Clementine there with me, too! Because important times are for friends, after all.

Maybe I wasn't *totally,* one hundred percent, fearless—yet.

But *actually,* I was definitely getting close!

Acknowledgments

A giant, Clementine-sized THANK YOU to: Debra Dorfman, for planting the seed; Lynn Weingarten, for watering it; Jodi Reamer, for sending Louise off and out with flying colors; Jill Gottlieb, for sharing her own childhood List of Scaredness Things; Judy Goldschmidt and Melissa Walker, for early reads and feedback; Brigette Barrager, for bringing Louise's world to life so perfectly and vividly; Nicole de las Heras and Elizabeth Tardiff, for the sparkly design; and Jenna Lettice and Alec Shane, for timely assistance. And an extra-extra-extra HURRAH to Michelle Nagler, as our professional relationship has now come full circle, delightfully (much like a hip circle over the flying trapeze—right?). Finally, thanks to my family, and most especially Noah and Mazzy, for keeping me young at heart.

About the Author

Fact: **MICOL OSTOW** is only about sixty-three percent fearless. Her List of Scaredness Things includes thunderstorms, ghost stories, and the pigeon that sits on top of her air conditioner and looks at her through her office window while she writes. (That pigeon's eyes are the beadiest!) She lives and works in Brooklyn, New York, with her husband, her daughter, and a small French bulldog that is *actually* a gigantic fraidy-cat. Learn more about Micol and Louise at micolostow.com.

About the Illustrator

BRIGETTE BARRAGER is an artist, illustrator, designer, and writer of children's books. She recently illustrated the *New York Times* bestseller *Uni the Unicorn* by Amy Krouse Rosenthal. She resides in Los Angeles with her handsome husband, cute doggy, and terrible cat. Visit Brigette at brigetteb.com.